FLOOD HAZARD

FLOOD HAZARD

MAURINE H. GEE

Illustrated by Charles Geer

William Morrow and Company   New York 1966

TABLE OF CONTENTS

ONE	Bicycle Trouble	9
TWO	Chester	20
THREE	More Trouble	31
FOUR	Buff Goes Native	38
FIVE	The Visitor	47
SIX	The Hunt	59
SEVEN	The Chase	69
EIGHT	The Orphan	76
NINE	Buff Hides Out	86
TEN	The Runaway	95
ELEVEN	The Flood	108
TWELVE	Doug and Buff	115

FLOOD
HAZARD

BICYCLE TROUBLE

CHAPTER ONE

On the way home from school Doug Markel dogtrotted along the sidewalk, trying to keep up with Stevie, who rode the bicycle. The bicycle belonged to Doug, but Stevie belonged to the Secret Six Club, and that made all the difference.

"What did Chuck Nars say about me joining the club?" Doug asked.

Stevie slowed down and trailed one foot along the cement curbing to keep his balance. "We've got to go easy," he said. "You're too new around here to do much pushing. First, you've got to get Chuck on your side."

"I've got you on my side," Doug reminded him.

"Sure," Stevie agreed. "But they only let me join because they wanted my TV set for their clubhouse."

That was the worst part about moving to a new school, Doug decided, no one knew you and no one wanted you around.

"Chuck says his dad is going to take all the Secret Six up to their mountain cabin during Christmas vacation," Stevie said. "There's supposed to be snow, and they've got a rack on top of their station wagon to carry skis and sleds and stuff."

Doug's longing to be one of the Secret Six grew and grew. "Sounds great," he said. He lifted his feet high at each step as he tried to imagine how it would feel to wade through deep snow. He had been born right there in Southern California, and the only snow he ever saw was on the distant mountaintops. "I'd sure like to go along," he said. "I'd sure like to wade in that snow."

"Who wouldn't?" said Stevie. He began to pump hard to get a start up the hill. "I've got to shove off. There's a meeting at the clubhouse."

Doug shifted his books from one arm to the other and hurried after him. "Wait," he called. "It's my turn on the bike."

Stevie pretended he didn't hear and kept right on going. Doug slowed down abruptly as he saw a familiar twosome headed his way—his neighbor, Mrs. Snead, and her boxer, Buff. Buff was a big square-built dog with short reddish hair, a white chest, a black mask, and the energy of a roller coaster. He liked to jump on Doug and get slobber marks all over his shirt.

Mrs. Snead was curious about Doug, because his parents were the new owners of the apartment building that was next door to her own little house. Every time she got near Doug, she tried to pump information from him.

No point in crossing to the far side of the street. She was sure to call to him, and he had to be polite. Ahead of him, off to the left, was a high cement retaining wall that marked the entrance of an alley. The alley promised a quick escape route, and Doug darted around the corner.

There was a yell and a screeching of tires as he slammed into a boy on a bicycle. Doug was knocked flat. He skidded along the asphalt making a clean sweep through dead leaves and grass cuttings. When he could get his breath, he sat up and looked around. Then he saw that the bicycle had smashed into the cement retaining wall.

The rider picked himself up from a litter of spilled books and papers, and turned to glare at Doug. It was Chuck Nars, the undisputed leader of the Secret Six. Doug groaned as he watched Chuck right his bicycle. Now *there* was a mess. The handlebars hung at a crazy angle and the front wheel was smashed, with the spokes sticking out every which way.

"Look what you've done," Chuck yelled, hoarse and angry. "You've got to pay to fix this bike. Every penny."

Stevie came wheeling in from the street and stopped suddenly. "What happened?" he cried.

Chuck turned on him as though he were responsible

for the accident. "Your fine friend wrecked my bike, that's what," he said. He studied Stevie more closely. "Where'd you get that bike?" he asked.

Stevie hesitated. He looked at Doug, opened his mouth and then closed it again without saying a word.

Slowly Doug got to his feet. "It's my bike," he said.

Chuck nodded. "Okay, Dud, so I use it until you get mine fixed," he said. He gestured to Stevie to call his attention to the scattered books and papers. "Bring my

stuff along," he said. "We don't want to be late for the meeting."

Stevie turned Doug's bicycle over to Chuck without a word of protest. As he gathered up Chuck's books and papers he glanced at Doug sideways. "You all right?" he asked.

Doug began to dust himself off. "I guess," he agreed.

"Well, that bike sure isn't," said Stevie.

He took off and Doug stood there with Chuck's bicycle at his feet. The front wheel would have to be rebuilt, at least ten dollars or more for labor, and the chrome rider that held the handlebars had to be straightened. Doug walked over and kicked the flat tire. Where in the world was he going to get the money to pay for all that repair work? Certainly not from his father, who didn't believe in handing out money free for nothing. All Doug would get out of him was that story about how far he used to walk to school when he was Doug's age. Perhaps his mother might . . . but no, she was sure to say, "We'll see what your father says."

Doug sighed. If he had to bump into someone, why did it have to be Chuck Nars? Now Chuck would be sore at him and not want him to join the Secret Six. Slowly Doug put his books in the paper carton on the back of Chuck's bike. He had to hold the wobbly front wheel up off the ground to get going. From there on it was an uphill climb, and he had to take it slowly.

He had forgotten Mrs. Snead and Buff, but there they were at the next corner. Mrs. Snead sat on the low cement wall that bordered the front lawn of the corner house. Doug thought it strange for her to be sitting there so quietly when she was supposed to be walking her dog. Her head was bent low and she was wheezing as though she had a bad cold. When Doug came along, she didn't even bother to glance up, but Buff pulled on his leash and wriggled all over in a friendly greeting.

"Sit," Mrs. Snead ordered, and Buff obeyed though his tongue lolled out and he seemed to be grinning at Doug.

"Will you do me a favor?" Mrs. Snead asked.

Doug balanced the bicycle on the kick stand, glad to take a breather. Mrs. Snead raised her head slowly, and Doug saw that her face looked as pasty as a biscuit that's ready for the oven.

"Could you leave your bike here and take Buff home for me?" she suggested, her voice low as though she hated to make the request. "I'll watch your bicycle while you're gone."

"Yes'm," Doug agreed hastily. Never before had he seen Mrs. Snead sitting hunched over that way, and never before had she asked a favor of him. "You want him put in the backyard?"

"Please," said Mrs. Snead. "Be sure to lock the gate."

Doug took the leash from her. Buff gave a yip of joy as he saw what was happening. Then he hunched his shoulders, stiffened his neck, and took off like a truck towing a feather. Doug was all but airborne. His feet slapped down on the walk every now and then as they raced along. He kept pulling back on the leash until both arms felt unhinged. The only thing that saved him from disaster was the fact that Buff's chain collar choked him and he had to slow down a time or two to get his breath.

It was three blocks to Cliffwood Road, the steep side

canyon where Doug lived in the Cliffwood Apartments, a two-story building. All the houses along Cliffwood Road were built on the hillside with one or two flights of steps to climb before you got to the front door.

Mrs. Snead's backyard was enclosed by a high board fence, and the fence was topped by three strands of barbed wire to keep Buff from sailing over the barrier. Doug had to stand on tiptoe to reach through a round hole in the wooden gate before he could release the catch and open the gate. Buff didn't mind being turned loose in his own yard, but he did hate to see Doug go off without him. He had been taught not to bark, but he whined in protest and threw himself against the gate.

Doug rubbed his aching arms with relief. Boy, was he ever glad he didn't have to trail along after that big moose every day. No wonder Mrs. Snead had given out on the job. That dog was enough to take the bounce out of anyone.

Doug glanced up at his own apartment building next door. He thought perhaps he should tell his mother about Mrs. Snead acting so queer before he went back to collect the bike. But likely his mother would be busy and certainly his little sister, Liza, would want to tag along. He felt that he had enough trouble on his hands without Liza.

He kept wondering what he was going to do about

Chuck's bike. If only he knew someone who owned a bicycle shop where they did repair work. He could work for them after school and make enough money to pay the repair bill. Or, if he were a little older, he could get a job as a box boy down at Jenkin's Market and have all the money he needed.

Slowly he walked back to Mrs. Snead and the bicycle.

"Thank you," she said with a friendly smile. "Now you can walk me home."

Slowly she got to her feet and walked along beside Doug. They were both puffing by the time they reached

her front walk. She put a hand on his shoulder and a spooky feeling went through him as he felt it tremble.

"Buff is a good dog," she said. "I owned his father and his father's father, and they were all fine pedigreed animals with wonderful dispositions. But Buff is so young and eager that he wears me out with his jerking and tugging. I tried boarding him at a nice kennel, but he wouldn't eat and got sick. I wonder if you would like to walk him for me every afternoon after school?"

As a matter of fact, Doug wouldn't like it at all. His arms still felt that they'd been pulled out six inches longer than usual. "I'm pretty busy after school," he said, careful to make it sound polite.

"Of course, I'd pay you for your trouble," said Mrs. Snead. "It shouldn't take more than an hour each day."

Doug stared at her. "You mean you'd pay me for walking Buff?" he asked in surprise.

Mrs. Snead nodded. "What would you think about fifty cents a day?" she asked.

Doug thought a great deal about it. Fifty cents seven times a week would be three dollars and fifty cents. Two weeks at three-fifty would be seven dollars, and from then on it wouldn't be any time at all until he had enough saved to pay for Chuck's bike.

"I could sure use the money," he admitted.

"Very well," said Mrs. Snead. "I'll expect you tomorrow after school."

She turned and went up her own walkway. Doug stared after her in sudden panic. What was going on here? Walk that elephant every afternoon? Was he out of his mind? He could hear Buff jumping against the side gate, thump, thump.

"Hey, wait a minute," he wanted to call after Mrs. Snead, but the sound was a mute inner cry. He dared not back out. He simply had to have that money.

CHAPTER TWO **CHESTER**

Doug hurried home to the apartment building next door. He took Chuck's bike up the narrow side steps and left it in the basement. He found his mother upstairs in the kitchen washing Liza's hair. The kitchen was really his bedroom, because they lived in two apartments that were singles. His dad's uncle had given him the apartment building, and now the Markels had to live there until they could sell it.

Mr. Markel had cut a door through the wall from the front apartment to the back apartment, and that left them with two kitchens. Doug had his choice. He could share his living room with Liza and sleep on the pull-out bed, or he could move a cot into the kitchen and have the whole place to himself. He chose the kitchen for his own.

Now he saw that all his things had been moved off

the sink to make room for Liza and her shampoo. She was stretched out on a big pink bath towel, her eyes squeezed shut to guard against any flying soapsuds.

Doug could feel himself swell with indignation. He hated to have people messing around with his things. Carefully he looked around to check on his pets. The friendly little red spider was still under the wire strainer on top of the stove. The two angel fish and the five guppies were swimming around the little castle in the aquarium. The light was on and the water was circulating with the proper sucking sound. But where was the brown paper carton?

"Where's Chester?" he asked in quick alarm.

Chester was the turtle he had found in the backyard of their other house. Chester was a beauty with sturdy, club-shaped feet and handsome markings on his brown shell. Someone had carved 1940 on the shell, and Doug had started to carve his initials under the date but, so far, he had nothing to show for his efforts except a nicked finger.

"Where's Chester? " he repeated.

His mother turned the rubber nozzle of the sprayer on Liza's hair. "I haven't seen Chester," she said. "Where did you leave him?"

"Right there on that sink," Doug said positively. He waited while his mother squeezed half of a fresh-smelling lemon into a glass of water and poured it over Liza's hair. But the moment Liza was in a sitting position he moved over to face her. "Liza," he said sternly, "what did you do with Chester?"

"I guess maybe he ran away," she said, opening one bright blue eye to see how Doug would take that information. "I guess maybe he's a naughty boy."

"Look who's talking," said Doug. "You know Chester is hibernating. I told you he won't wake up till he's good and ready."

"Emily says he must eat his lettuce," said Liza. "Emily told him and told him to wake up and eat his lettuce."

Emily was the big floppy rag doll that Liza carried around with her. Emily was almost as big as Liza. She had black yarn hair and she wore a red and white dress that Liza had outgrown. She had been left on the lawn a time or two, and there she was soaked by the sprinklers and bleached by the sun. She looked like something that belonged in a rag bag, but to Liza she was the most beautiful doll in the world.

Doug appealed to his mother. "Mom, can't you make Liza stay out of my things?"

"I thought you were going to dig a hole outside for Chester," said his mother.

"I am," said Doug, "as soon as I finish carving my initials on his shell."

"This time carve the shell and not your finger," cautioned Mrs. Markel. She ran a comb through Liza's hair, leaving a mass of damp ringlets. "Now, Miss Nosey, what did you do with Chester?"

Liza giggled. She got down from the sink holding tightly to Emily. She scrambled under Doug's bed and shoved Chester's paper carton out into the open.

"See, he wouldn't eat," she said, eyeing the wilted lettuce leaf that lay on the burlap sack that covered Chester. "He's naughty not to eat his lunch."

Doug saw that he had to do something about Chester. Initials or no initials, he had to get busy and make a decent hideout for his pet. Anything to keep him out of Liza's clutches. And he would see to it that she didn't know where Chester's burrow was located. The less Liza knew, the less trouble she would cause. Gently Doug lifted Chester's box.

"I'll help you," Liza cried with gusto. "Wait till I get Emily's buggy."

She hurried to the other room. Desperately Doug appealed to his mother. "Please keep her here," he urged. "If she sees where I put Chester, she's sure to dig him up."

"Go ahead," Mrs. Markel agreed. "Be sure to put a marker so you'll know where to find him."

"Don't worry, he'll find himself when the time

comes," said Doug. "He'll climb out ready to eat everything in sight." At that moment he remembered what it was he wanted to tell his mother. "You know that Mrs. Snead who lives next door," he said. "Well, she's going to pay me fifty cents a day to walk her dog."

"Mrs. Snead?" said Mrs. Markel in surprise. "She told me she enjoys walking her dog."

"I guess he's getting to be too much for her," said Doug, doubling his fists to make his muscles bulge. "I need the money on account of I sort of wrecked a kid's bike."

"You what?" Mrs. Markel gave him her full attention. "You ran into someone?" she said.

"Nope," said Doug. "He ran into me."

"Then it must have been his fault," said Mrs. Markel, sounding relieved.

"Not this guy," said Doug. "He's a big shot at school. Nothing is ever his fault. He calls all the answers and that's the way it is."

"Not with me, it isn't," said Mrs. Markel firmly. "What happened to your bike?"

"Nothing," said Doug. "I'm just letting this Chuck ride it until I can get his bike fixed."

Mrs. Markel was not satisfied with the explanation. "Doug, are you letting some bully boss you around?" she asked.

Doug faced her, his eyes wide. "I told you it was my fault," he said. "This Chuck is okay, I guess. His dad owns half the stores on the boulevard, and he's head of the best club at school. Maybe he has a right to be sore. If it wasn't for me, his bike wouldn't be wrecked."

"Where is this wreck?" asked Mrs. Markel.

"In our basement," said Doug. "You can go down and see for yourself."

"That's not in my department," said Mrs. Markel. "You'll have to take that up with your father."

Doug sighed. Worry, worry, that's all he ever did around here. He took Chester to the basement and got a shovel. Outside he chose a nice spot for Chester, a shady place on the down slope next to Mrs. Snead's fence. Buff heard him digging there and came charging over to see what was going on. He whined and dug furiously on his side of the fence. But the fence was sturdy, and he didn't get far.

Doug was still digging when Stevie came by. Stevie lived with his mother and father in the double apartment across the hallway from Doug's.

"Thought you were going to the Secret Six meeting," said Doug.

"I left early," said Stevie. "I'm worried about what you're going to do with Chuck's bike."

"Yeah." Doug had to grin. "It's going to be tough on you having that long walk to school."

Stevie didn't see the joke. "I mean Chuck said to tell you to get a move on. He wants his bike back, good as new, and no waiting around."

That waiting around was the part that worried Doug, but he wasn't going to admit it. "I've got everything under control," he said. "I've got a job."

Stevie seemed to think this statement was another joke. "What kind of a job?" he asked.

Doug hesitated. "It's something that pays me fifty cents a day," he said.

"What pays fifty cents a day?" Stevie asked.

"Something," said Doug.

"Aw, come on, tell me what it is," Stevie urged. "I'm your best friend."

Doug grunted as he dug more dirt from Chester's hole. "Oh, sure. And who turned my bike over to Chuck?" he asked. "Is that any way to be a friend?"

Stevie tried again. "It's just that I know how you feel about joining the Secret Six," he said. "I don't want Chuck sore at you."

Doug couldn't argue with that. He shrugged and Stevie brightened, quick to change the subject. "Why you digging that hole?" he asked.

Doug tried to be patient. Stevie had eyes in his head. He could see Chester's box right there as plain as day. "I'll give you two guesses," he said.

"Guess it must be winter quarters for Chester," Stevie said. "You going to put those old papers in with him?"

"Nope," Doug said. He scraped a soft litter of dead leaves from under the abelia bush and spread it over the bottom of the hole. "Over at our other house I used pine needles for his bed, but I guess these leaves will do."

"Why sure," Stevie agreed.

Chester had withdrawn from the world, not even a toenail showed. Doug placed him gently in the hole and covered him with more leaves. Then he filled the hole with dirt.

"Doesn't he have to breathe?" Stevie asked.

Doug shrugged. "All I know is they have lungs and they breathe, but not like us. My dad says their top shell is really their ribs all grown together."

He got a flower stake from the basement and drove it into the ground near Chester. "There! Now I won't forget where I left him."

Stevie glanced up at the side windows of his apartment. "I've got to go," he said. "Mom's calling me."

Sure enough, there stood his mother at the window motioning to him. He hurried inside, and Doug returned the shovel to its place in the basement. The moment he got back upstairs his mother reminded him to get busy on his homework. He got busy all right, busy worrying about what kind of a deal he could make with his dad. Maybe his dad would pay for having Chuck's bike fixed right away. Then Doug could pay him back at the rate of three-fifty a week. Maybe his dad would agree to the plan, and then again maybe he wouldn't. Doug sighed. If there was a delay, Chuck was going to get sore and he would see to it that Doug never got to join the Secret Six. And on top of everything else, Doug had to admit that it was a long, long walk to school.

MORE TROUBLE

CHAPTER THREE

Doug's mother called to him, "I wish you'd take Liza outside while I get dinner."

Liza refused to leave the apartment until she had her doll buggy crammed full of treasures: a moth-eaten panda, a scuffed red purse, a faded blue blanket, and a pair of green satin slippers with sparkly high heels that made her a grownup the minute she stepped into them. Poor old Emily rode on top of the heap.

Liza wheeled the buggy out to the hallway. At the front door she began to yell, "Help me! Help me!"

Her doll buggy was caught between the front door and the jamb. Doug freed the buggy and started to take it down the front steps.

"Let me," cried Liza. "I'll do it myself."

Oh boy, that Liza. She was either yelling for help or she was fighting him off.

When their mother called them inside, Doug began to watch the clock. His dad was supposed to be home for dinner by six o'clock. But tonight he was late. Doug listened for the familiar putt putt of the station wagon as it went up the driveway, and all the while he kept rehearsing what he was going to say. He never did hear the car, but he heard his dad at the front door as his key rattled in the lock.

Liza heard it too. The minute Mr. Markel got the door opened, she ran to him and threw herself into his arms. He picked her up and pretended to listen to her babble about Emily, but he was really looking over her curly head and smiling at Mrs. Markel.

"Good news," he said. "You remember that Mr. Evans who looked at the apartments last Saturday?"

Mrs. Markel nodded.

"Sure," said Doug hurriedly. "He's the one who kept pounding the walls and asking the tenants if they'd seen any termites lately."

"That's the man," said Mr. Markel. "He came to my office this afternoon and said he wants to buy this place."

Mrs. Markel let out a faint cry of joy. "Really?" she said.

"Keep your fingers crossed," said Mr. Markel. "May I eat and run? I promised to be at his house by seven o'clock. I've got to talk to his wife. It seems she's the one who has the money."

Mrs. Markel rushed to the kitchen. "Hurry," she called back. "I'll have everything on the table by the time you've washed up."

Doug started to follow his father to the bathroom, anxious to get the burden of Chuck's bicycle off his mind. But his mother called to him. "Don't bother your father now," she said. "Believe me, this is no time to mention that bicycle. Put the milk on the table, and we're ready to eat."

Doug was a fast eater, but this was one time he couldn't keep up with his dad. He hadn't finished half his mound of mashed potatoes when his father excused himself and took off. Doug tried to be patient. He told himself he would have to wait and corner his dad the moment he got back. He was sure to see Chuck at school tomorrow and he had to have something definite to tell him. Chuck hadn't been fooling when he sent that message by Stevie. He wanted action on that bike of his and he wanted it now.

At eight-thirty the familiar call came from his mother, "Take your shower, Doug. Brush your teeth and get to bed."

"Can't I wait up till Dad gets back?" he begged.

"No," said Mrs. Markel. "He may be quite late."

Doug turned the water on in his shower so his mother would hear it running. She wasn't the kind who told you to do something and then forgot about it. He undressed and stood in the doorway of the shower, one foot thrust forward to feel the sting of the spray. After thinking it over, he decided he would not bother to get wet all over. He hated all that work later when he tried to get dry enough so his pajamas wouldn't stick to him.

The water was making so much noise that he didn't hear his mother come in. Firmly she pushed him in under the cascade of water. Then she handed him a sweet-smelling cake of soap and a washcloth. "Scrub those ears," she said.

Doug leaned out of the waterfall, blinking against the spray. "Can't a person have any privacy around here?" he demanded.

"Certainly," said Mrs. Markel. "But first he has to get his neck and ears clean."

Doug groaned. He closed the glass door and turned his back to the spray. The water peppered down just right. Actually, once he got wet, he found that tingly feeling wasn't so bad. Not bad at all. He faced the spray and opened his mouth to let the water ping against his teeth. And that reminded him of a certain tiresome chore. Quickly he scrubbed his teeth with the washcloth. Nothing like saving wear and tear on his toothbrush.

Presently his mother knocked on the shower door. Doug turned off the water and stuck his head out the door. "Is Dad back?" he asked.

"No," said his mother, handing him a bath towel, "but you've been in there long enough."

"If I can't talk to Dad," said Doug, "what am I going to tell Chuck?"

"You'll think of something," said his mother. "You're good at that."

She left and Doug mopped at himself. He got into his pajamas and they stuck to him just as he knew they would. He crawled into bed and lay there worrying about what he was going to tell Chuck. He kept on worrying until he decided to get up early in the morning and let his father decide what ought to be done. His father was the one who should make the decision. All Doug had to do was to wake up extra early in the morning.

His inner alarm clock failed to go off. He didn't know a thing the next morning until he felt his mother shaking his shoulder. "Doug, get up," she was saying. "Hurry, or you'll be late for school."

Doug was so sleepy that he was eating his grapefruit before the memory of Chuck's bike fell on him with a nasty thud. "Where's Dad?" he asked.

"He left early," said Mrs. Markel.

Doug was still groggy, but not too groggy to know catastrophe when it hit him. "What am I going to tell Chuck?" he demanded.

"I'm afraid I don't know," said his mother cheerfully.

"But you're no worse off than you were the last time we discussed it."

Doug glanced at her suspiciously, but she wasn't smiling as she poured milk on Liza's cereal. Mostly she was dependable, but there were times when she seemed to be smiling privately to herself. "I don't see what's to be so happy about," he said.

His mother crossed two of her fingers and held them up for him to see. "It's just that I'm so anxious to get rid of these apartments," she said. "It's no place for children."

"But, Mom, we've only been here since school started."

His mother stared at him. "You mean to say you like it here?" she asked. "You mean to say you like sleeping in a kitchen?"

Doug shrugged. "Sometimes yes and sometimes no," he said. "I thought you told Dad you were not going to transfer me to any other school this year," he reminded her. "You said one change a semester was enough."

"Don't worry," said Mrs. Markel. "We plan to stay in this neighborhood. There are some lovely homes over on Shady Oak Drive."

Doug glanced at the clock and caught up his books.

"He hasn't brushed his teeth," Liza cried in triumph.

"Oh boy," said Doug wearily. "I can see this is going to be one of those days."

CHAPTER FOUR **BUFF GOES NATIVE**

Stevie walked to school with Doug. They had gone only a couple of blocks before Chuck Nars went swishing by on Doug's bicycle. He slowed down to let them catch up with him.

"Hey, Dud," he called, "this hunk of junk you ride should be put out to pasture."

Doug hated to be called Dud, but he forced a smile. "That's right," he said. "Leave it right there. I'll be glad to take it off your hands."

"Very funny," said Chuck, not at all amused. "When do I get my bike?"

"Soon as I get the green light from my dad," said Doug.

"What's wrong?" Chuck asked. "What's the delay?"

Doug moved on a step or two. "I didn't get a chance to

talk to him," he said. "I'll straighten it out tonight."

Chuck scowled and turned to Stevie. "What goes on here?" he asked. "Didn't you deliver my message?"

"Sure I told him," Stevie said. "I told him you wanted an instant repair job."

"And what did he say?" Chuck asked, as though Doug weren't even there.

Stevie glanced uneasily from Chuck to Doug and then back again. "He said he had a job and there would be no problem," he said.

"Ha," said Chuck, as though he doubted any such nonsense. "What kind of a job?"

"He didn't say," Stevie admitted.

Chuck turned to Doug. "All right," he said, "what is this job you're so proud of?"

Doug felt there were some questions that were better left unanswered. For all he knew Chuck might try to horn in on walking Buff. He might go to Mrs. Snead and offer to walk her dog for half price.

"It's nothing to talk about," Doug said. "It's just a little gold mine I have tucked away. . . . Hey, come on, Stevie, we're going to be late."

Chuck let them go, but he kept haunting Doug all the rest of the day. There seemed to be dozens of him popping up on the playground, in the cafeteria, or in the washroom. No matter where Doug went, Chuck was sure to show up with some of his friends. He kept asking questions about Doug's mysterious job. He thought it was funny to make a guessing game of it.

"Could be you're selling fresh eggs from door to door?" he asked. "I'll bet you'd lay a dandy egg. If I'm getting close, if I'm getting hot, it's only fair to tell me."

"Oh, you're hot as a firecracker," Doug assured him.

Chuck winked at one of his friends. "Aw, come on, Dud. You always want to be so friendly, why not let us in on the secret?"

Through all the ribbing, Doug managed to keep from boiling over. As long as Chuck was the big shot with the Secret Six, he had everything his own way. He was just looking for an excuse to keep Doug out of the club. Stevie and the other club members liked Doug well enough. It was his hard luck that they all followed Chuck's lead, no matter who was left out.

Secretly, Doug was fed up with Chuck's everlasting questions and that afternoon after school, when he saw Stevie and Chuck crowding around the blue ice-cream truck at the corner, he walked two blocks out of his way to avoid them.

He reached home so winded that he could scarcely speak. Liza stared at him with big round eyes. "What chased you?" she asked.

"A fierce dragon," Doug told her obligingly.

Liza hugged Emily to her and squealed with delight. "Is he hiding in the hallway?" she asked.

"I wouldn't be surprised," said Doug, putting his books down and heading for the cooky jar.

He was on his second walnut cooky, washing it down with a glass of milk, when the telephone rang. His mother answered. "Yes," she said, "he just came in. . . . Yes, thank you, I'll tell him it's hanging on the nail beside the back door."

Doug sighed. Here he was so tired he could scarcely breathe, and yet Mrs. Snead wasn't willing to let him rest for five minutes before he took that dog of hers for a walk.

"I'll bet that was Mrs. Snead," he said. "She's afraid I'll forget to walk her dog."

"No, it was her nurse," said Mrs. Markel. "Mrs. Snead is sick in bed and she wants you to know that the dog's leash is hanging on a nail by the back door."

"No hurry," said Doug. "I can walk him any time."

"I will go too," sang out Liza. "I will walk Emily in her buggy."

Now there was a beautiful thought, that elephant of a dog getting his leash all tangled around that beat-up doll buggy.

"Oh no, you don't," Doug said. "I'll have my hands full without you and that Emily."

He gulped the last of his milk and hurried out before Liza worked up a storm.

Buff was anxious and well-behaved until Doug got him outside of Mrs. Snead's yard. Then, sure that he was off for a walk, he gave a woof of joy and took off down the hill, headed along the usual route of his afternoon walk, which was sure to lead to a meeting with Chuck and Stevie.

Doug didn't want to see either one of them and he tried to turn Buff around and head him back up the hill. Buff did not care to retrace his steps. He hunched down against the choke of his collar and continued on his way. He dragged Doug along after him until he paused to

sniff at the base of a green lamppost. Doug was quick to wrap the leash around the post, and there he held Buff until the dog quieted down and lost that wild look in his eyes. Then, by half-sitting on the leash when Buff pulled too hard, Doug managed to turn him around and head him back up the hill.

Presently they were in the upper canyon, territory that was new to Doug. They passed a sign that read, *Dead End Street,* and went on until the houses gave out and the sidewalk ended. They walked along the worn black-top, which became a dirt road. The road was nicely shaded with trees and the dry air smelled of eucalyptus leaves and pine needles.

The canyon narrowed, and they came to a tall steel mesh fence, where their way was barred by a sturdy double gate. A chain and padlock held the gates closed, and a big sign read, *Cliffwood Reservoir. No Trespassing.*

Beyond the gate the two ruts of the road turned to the left and disappeared in a growth of hillside brush. Straight ahead there was a great fill of earth, as tall as a three-story building. It was a dam filling in the gap be-tween two hills that were a part of the mountain slope.

Doug thought of the hundreds of truckloads of earth it must have taken to build the dam. He could imagine the long string of dump trucks, some red, some yellow, some blue, creeping up Cliffwood, right past his own apartment building, like ants headed for a pile of sugar. Or maybe the dam builders had used big earthmovers to scoop out the mountainside to get enough dirt and rocks to make the big fill. Doug wished he had lived here when all the excitement was going on.

Buff sat down on his haunches in front of the gate and looked back over his shoulder at Doug, waiting for him to open the gate so they could continue on their walk. Doug rattled the lock and chain, trying to show him that the gate was not about to open and that this was as far as they could go.

"Down, Buff," he said sternly, trying to sound as firm as Mrs. Snead. "Lie down!"

He sat down on a big flat rock to give Buff the idea. The dog settled down in the dirt beside him, panting hard, his eyes half-closed and his tongue dripping. Doug didn't care much for Buff's display of teeth. They were white and even, but they looked sharp enough and strong enough to crunch a steak bone like peanut brittle. Doug reminded himself that Buff's father and his father's father had wonderful dispositions. Mrs. Snead had said so and certainly she ought to know.

A blue jay lit in the branch of a wild cherry across the road and scolded at them for coming where they were not invited. There was a skittering movement in the brush back of Doug, and a rabbit shot past them and bounced across the road. Buff sprang after the rabbit with a yip of excitement. The leash jerked from Doug's hand, and Buff raced after the rabbit, gaining on him at every jump.

Doug yelled and ran after him. One snap of Buff's jaws and it would be the end of that rabbit. Suddenly the rabbit jerked to one side and dived through a hole that went under the fence. Buff couldn't stop. He slammed into the fence and landed in a scrambling heap. Safe on the far side of the fence, the rabbit kept on running as though he still felt Buff's hot breath on his neck.

Buff got to his feet and began to dig like mad trying to enlarge the rabbit's escape tunnel. He straddled the trail and dug with his forepaws, sending out a great shower of dirt and stones. In a frenzy of impatience he tried to push himself through the hole. Only his nose could make it, but he kept turning and twisting trying to force his way through. Finally, winded and exhausted, he backed away and shook himself.

Looking like a clown with his nose and eyes all white with dust, he whined and turned to Doug for help. "Don't look at me," Doug said sternly. "I'm all for the rabbit." He caught up the leash and pulled Buff back to the flat rock. "Sit!" he ordered, and he gave the leash three short jerks to let Buff know that he meant what he said. "No chasing the bunnies," he said.

Buff seemed to get the message. His ears flattened and he ducked his head, as though he understood that rabbit chasing was strictly forbidden. And yet he trembled and drooled as he looked through the fence and eyed the spot where the rabbit had disappeared.

"You don't need to think that bunny is coming back," Doug told him. "He's not *that* stupid."

Buff whined and pulled at the leash, anxious to get back to his digging.

Doug was disgusted. "Come on, we may as well go home," he said. "What's the good of coming up here where it's all nice and quiet when all you can think about is catching rabbits?"

Buff held back. He didn't want to leave. He was sure a nice juicy rabbit would spring out at them any moment now. He kept holding back all the way down the hill until they reached the sidewalk and the light standards, where some new smells got his mind off the rabbit.

Doug decided that was the last time he would take Buff up the hill. He had no sympathy for a dog that wanted to gobble up every rabbit he saw. Mrs. Snead might think she had a sweet well-mannered animal on her hands, but today Buff had shown all the instincts of a killer.

"Don't whine at me," he told Buff, as he shut him up in Mrs. Snead's backyard. "You're just not my kind of a dog."

CHAPTER FIVE **THE VISITOR**

When Mr. Markel drove into the garage that evening, Doug was waiting. "I sure wish you'd take a look at Chuck's bike and see what ought to be done about it," he said.

His father followed him to the basement and stood looking at the bicycle while Doug did some hasty explaining.

"I know," said Mr. Markel. "Your mother told me you're walking Mrs. Snead's dog to make enough to pay for the repairs."

"Saving up the money will take too long," said Doug. "I thought maybe we could make a deal. I thought maybe you'd take the bike to Runkle's tomorrow morning and get them to fix it. Then I'll pay you back as soon as I get the money from Mrs. Snead."

Mr. Markel turned away. "Afraid not," he said. *"You*

take the bicycle to Runkle's when you've saved the money to pay for it."

"Chuck won't wait," Doug protested.

"He has your bike, hasn't he?"

Doug nodded.

"Then he has no complaint," said Mr. Markel.

The firm way he spoke warned Doug that this was no time to press the matter. Quietly Doug followed his father up the basement stairs to the lower hallway and their own apartment. He kept wondering what in the world he was going to tell Chuck.

Mrs. Markel met them at the front door. She was smiling and eager. "Did they sign up?" she asked. "Are we going to sell?"

Mr. Markel glanced down at the newspaper he carried. "I'm afraid the deal's off," he said. "No sale."

Mrs. Markel couldn't believe it. "What happened?" she cried.

"Evans claims he didn't know the Cliffwood Reservoir is in the hills above us," said Mr. Markel. "He says it's a flood hazard."

Mrs. Markel's eyes widened with indignation. "He just wants you to come down on the price," she said. "Surely he knows the city engineers would never permit anyone to build a dam that wasn't safe."

"Don't worry," said Mr. Markel. "We'll find another buyer."

Doug went into the next room. Liza lay on the floor beside her doll buggy, busy swiping a yellow crayon across a page in her coloring book. Sky, ship, and birds were all turning a bright yellow.

"Unpack your doll buggy," Doug told her cheerfully. "We're not going to move."

Liza rolled over and sat up. "Who says?" she asked.

"I say," Doug told her.

Liza giggled. She got up and fished Emily from the overstuffed buggy. "Come on, Emily," she said, "Daddy's home."

After supper Mr. Markel called to Doug, "Come on, this is the night we put out the trash barrels."

Every Friday evening the barrels had to be taken from the basement and lined up along the curbing in front of the apartment house. Then, Saturday morning, a big white truck came rumbling along and picked up the trash.

Doug held the hand truck in place while his dad loaded on each barrel. It took eight trips to get all the barrels out in front. By the time the last one was neatly lined up, Doug had thought up another way to raise some money.

"Think I'll go over and ask Mrs. Snead if she won't pay me in advance," he told his father. "Later I can walk Buff for free a couple of times to pay her back, like paying interest on the money."

Mr. Markel shook his head. "Forget it," he said. "Mrs. Snead is sick and you're not to bother her. Do you understand?"

"Yes, sir," said Doug, and there went another brilliant plan down the drain. And yet he couldn't resist one last effort. "I sure hate to face Chuck Nars tomorrow," he said.

Mr. Markel said nothing.

Despite all Doug's worries, Friday turned out to be a satisfactory day. Chuck Nars did not show up at school. There had been an unexpected snowfall in the mountains, and Stevie reported that Chuck and his family had gone to Lake Arrowhead to get in some skiing. At least, when they left, Stevie had seen a bunch of skis in the carrier on top of their station wagon.

"People in California have to take their snow when they can get it," said Stevie. "Boy, I sure wish I could go with them."

Doug knew what he meant. All day long he drifted around feeling lighter than air. He loved his school, he loved his teachers, and he loved his new friends. It was a fine experience to go his own way with no interference from Chuck Nars.

That afternoon, when it came time to walk Buff, Doug took a firm grip on the leash and started off down the hill, thinking Buff would be delighted to travel his old route again. But no, Buff had other ideas. From the moment they left his yard he was determined to take the quickest route back up the canyon to that magic spot where wild rabbits jumped out at him.

Doug tugged on the leash, trying to head Buff downhill, but Buff turned his back and braced himself. He weighed seventy pounds or more, and he wouldn't budge until Doug gave in and allowed himself to be pulled up the hill. Doug dug his heels into the ground and made himself as heavy as possible. Buff had to stop every so often to get his wind, and each time he stopped he glanced back over his shoulder as though wondering how Doug got all that lead in his shoes. Doug wanted to make it plain that he was dead set against Buff's chasing rabbits. He wanted Buff to understand that he was on the rabbit's side, no question about that.

There were fresh tire marks on the dirt road, which meant that a city truck or an inspector had been up this way. One moment Doug was looking at the tire marks, and the next moment he was jerked off his feet and the dirt road heaved up and hit him in the face. He scrambled to his knees in time to see Buff tearing off after three rabbits that sprang out from a cover of wild oats and raced for the fence.

The leaping rabbits, their long ears laid back out of the way, fanned out in three directions. Buff was practically on top of them. He could have caught any one of them if he hadn't been so greedy. But he didn't want just one, he wanted all three of them. He raced from one to the other, shifting and swerving, until all three got away. Each found a different escape hole under the fence and tore away on the far side.

Again and again Buff threw himself at the fence. He even forgot his special training and barked in a frenzy of protest. Doug got hold of his leash and pulled until he got him back on the road. Some day that crazy dog was going to catch one of those rabbits and tear it to pieces. Doug cringed at the thought. There ought to be some way to warn the rabbits. The next time Buff dragged him up this way, he would start to whistle long before they got there, and if those rabbits had any sense they would vanish before Buff got near them.

Saturday morning Mrs. Markel made some of her special baked custard to take to Mrs. Snead. "The nurse says she won't eat," Mrs. Markel told Doug, who stood in the kitchen drooling over the smell of vanilla and nutmeg. "Take Liza out to play. I won't be gone long."

Of course, Liza had to take Emily and the doll buggy along. Then she got busy wheeling the buggy around and around one of the acacia trees that grew next to the curbing. Doug amused himself by throwing his baseball far up the sidewalk and letting it roll back again.

Doug was getting a real workout until his ball got stuck behind one of the trash barrels. As he bent to get it, he glanced down the street and saw Chuck Nars headed up the hill. Chuck, who was supposed to be up in the mountains, was actually down there at the corner heading this way. Doug was sure he meant to raise a rumpus over his bicycle. Quickly Doug crouched down behind the nearest barrel, and he pulled Liza down beside him.

She squawked, but Doug put a hand over her mouth. "Sh," he whispered. "Here comes Wicked Wang. We've got to hide."

Liza quit struggling and made herself as small as possible. "Where is he?" she wanted to know.

"Sh," warned Doug, his lips close to her ear. "He hasn't seen us yet."

Liza giggled. She loved to play scary games. "Where is he now?" she asked.

"Going up the front steps," said Doug. "When he goes inside, we'll sneak in the garage. Sh, don't move. I'll tell you when."

Chuck went up the steps in as businesslike a way as if he were someone collecting for his paper route. The moment he was inside the house, Doug quickly caught Liza's hand and rushed her up the ramp into the garage.

Quietly they crept up the basement stairs that led to the front hallway. Cautiously Doug opened the door a crack. Chuck stood at the Markels' door, his thumb pressed on the doorbell. No one answered the ring, and yet he stood there with his thumb pressed to the bell.

Liza knelt down and crowded in at Doug's feet to peer through the crack. "He's no Wicked Wang," she complained in a whisper. "He's a boy."

Doug closed the door, careful not to make a sound.

"Wicked Wang tries to fool people," he explained. "He tries to look human."

"Let me see," Liza begged.

Doug wouldn't take a chance until he heard the front door open and close. He cautioned Liza to stay back out of sight while he went to look out through the glass panel of the front door. Chuck was sitting on the grass beside the trash barrels; he looked as though he meant to camp there the rest of the day.

Doug took Liza into their apartment and quieted her down with a rambling story that he stretched to outlast Chuck. "Once upon a time there was this sappy princess," he began as an opener.

Liza wriggled down on the sofa beside him. "And her name was Liza," she said with satisfaction. "She was a beautiful princess."

"She just thought she was beautiful," Doug corrected. "That's because old Wicked Wang had sprayed her mirror with no-truth goo."

"So, she's beautiful," Liza insisted, impatient to get on with the story. "Is she locked up in the castle with no bridge table down?"

"You mean drawbridge," said Doug. "I guess that's about it. There was this creepy princess locked up in the castle with a drawbridge that needed the axe."

Entertaining Liza was a cinch. All Doug had to do was to supply a thought or two, and she filled in the details. He went to the window every so often to check on Chuck Nars. Chuck was a stayer. He held out through several princess adventures plus the time it took Doug to go to the kitchen and whip up a froth of chocolate milk. Chuck stuck it out while the trash collectors thumped the barrels around, and then he hung around some more. Doug was beginning to feel cooped up before Chuck finally headed for home.

Doug gave him plenty of time to get away. He didn't

want him hiding out at the next corner ready to pounce out the moment Doug appeared. "Let's go," he told Liza. "Old Wicked Wang has gone."

They went down the front steps, and Liza began to search around the trash barrels. "Where's Emily?" she cried in alarm. "Where's her buggy?"

"Don't get excited," said Doug. "It has to be around here somewhere."

Liza stood on tiptoe to peer into the empty trash barrels. She examined them one by one. Even Doug had to admit there was no buggy there.

Liza squeezed her eyes shut and began to bellow. "That Wicked Wang ran off with Emily."

"No such thing," said Doug. "I saw him leave. He didn't have a buggy with him and he didn't have Emily."

"He used magic," Liza wailed. She pounced on a shiny lid from a pickle jar that had fallen into the gutter. "He made my dolly into a bottle top."

"Don't be silly," Doug begged.

The sound of Liza's wailing brought their mother out on the porch of Mrs. Snead's house. "What's wrong?" she called, hurrying toward them. "What happened?"

At the sight of her mother, Liza raced toward her bellowing louder than ever. Mrs. Markel picked her up and turned to Doug for an explanation.

"Don't worry," he said. "She's not hurt."

"Old Wicked Wang took my Emily," Liza said between sobs. "My buggy and all my things are gone."

"What happened?" Mrs. Markel repeated.

Doug didn't know and he hated to mention the suspicion that occurred to him. "Her things were right here," he said. "Do you suppose the trash collectors could have taken them?"

"Don't you know?" Mrs. Markel asked sharply. "Where were you?"

"In the house," Doug said. Before he thought he added, "Chuck Nars was here, he would know."

"Then go call him," said Mrs. Markel. "Ask him if the rubbish collectors took a doll buggy."

A chill went through Doug. "I can't do that," he protested. "I've been hiding out from the guy all morning. I wouldn't call him for fifty million dollars."

Mrs. Markel started up the front steps with Liza. "Then I'll call him," she said.

Doug groaned. He knew good and well he wasn't going to talk to Chuck, and yet what kind of a chicken would he be if he let his mother do the calling. Worry, worry, that's all he ever did around here.

CHAPTER SIX **THE HUNT**

Reluctantly Doug followed his mother to their apartment. "Get busy and phone Chuck," she said.

An angry feeling began to swell up inside him. "I can't," he protested. "You can't expect me to call him when I spent all morning hiding from him. It isn't fair."

"Fair or not," said Mrs. Markel, "Liza has a right to know what happened to Emily and her buggy."

Doug hated to touch that telephone. Slowly he dialed Chuck's number. He hoped no one would answer. He kept hoping no one would be home until he heard Chuck's hearty voice.

He had to swallow twice before he could get out a word. "This is Doug Markel," he said. "Were you up at my house when the trash truck came by?"

"Ha, you know darned good and well I was there," Chuck said.

"Look," Doug said, "my little sister is bawling her head off because someone took her doll buggy. Did the trash man take it?"

"I thought it belonged to you," said Chuck with a snicker. "Sure, the buggy was right there with all the other junk and when one of the guys asked, 'Does this buggy go too?' I said it sure did on account of you were too big to play with dolls."

Doug had expected some such corny humor, but he had no time to argue. "You mean the trash collectors took the buggy?" he asked.

"Yep," said Chuck.

"Which way did the truck go?" Doug asked.

"How do I know?" said Chuck. "I'm no detective."

"Forget it," Doug said.

"Just a minute there," said Chuck. "I want to know what you've done with my bike."

Doug hesitated only a moment and then gently, very gently, he eased the receiver back into place. "The truck took the buggy," he told his mother. "Now what?"

"Go find it," she said promptly, "and get the men to return Liza's things."

She made it sound as simple as bringing in the evening paper, but Doug didn't even know where to start. "Where am I supposed to look?" he asked. "The truck's been gone a long time."

"Look up and down the side streets," said his mother. "Take your bike."

"I don't have my bike," he reminded her.

"Then walk," she said.

Doug went outside. He hurried down to the corner. He looked up the street and he looked down the street, but there was no sign of the big white truck. He climbed up on the retaining wall of the corner house to look up and down the side street and still there was no sign of the truck.

When he got back to the apartment, he found his mother trying to get Liza to take her nap. "I want my Emily," Liza cried. She had been crying so long that each sob sounded like a hiccup.

Mrs. Markel took Liza in her arms and moved over to the rocking chair. "Sh, darling," she said softly. "Doug will find your Emily. Sh, close your eyes."

Doug shrugged. "No truck," he told his mother. "It just disappeared."

Mrs. Markel remained calm. "It couldn't disappear," she said. "Somewhere in this town some rubbish collector has Emily and that buggy. It's up to you to get on the telephone and find out where it is."

She might as well have asked him to check on the flight of a migrating hummingbird. "Who am I supposed to call?" he asked.

"Look in the front pages of the telephone directory," she said. "Call City Hall. Ask the switchboard operator to connect you with the department of sanitation or the rubbish collectors."

"But suppose—"

Liza had quieted down to listen, but now she started up again, and Mrs. Markel waved Doug toward the door. "Just do your best," she said. "I'm depending on you."

Doug looked up City Hall in the telephone book. His hands felt clammy as he picked up the phone and dialed the number.

"City Hall," said a brisk feminine voice.

"Look," said Doug, trying to make his voice sound deep. "I want to speak to the trash collectors' department."

"Sorry," said the lady. "All city offices are closed on Saturdays."

A feeling of desperation swept over Doug. "But my sister is yelling her head off because they took her doll and her doll buggy that was parked in front of our house. Will they burn it or what?"

"Sorry," said the lady, "I do not have that information." There was a brief pause. "However," she added in a softer tone, "I suggest you report the loss to the police department. Perhaps they can help you."

"Yes, ma'am," said Doug, and he hung up before he remembered to thank her. He was too busy thinking about Si Bartlett, the only person he knew on the police force. Every school day, mornings and afternoons, Si sat in a black and white patrol car in the shade of a big pine tree on Fifth Street to watch the school crossings. He had been the speaker at a school assembly about safety rules, and he was nice and friendly when Doug was the crossing guard.

This being a Saturday, Si would be down on the boulevard cruising along or he would be parked near one of the crossing lights to keep an eye on the traffic. Doug felt sure Si would try to help him.

Liza had quieted down. Doug went to her room and saw that her eyes were closed. His mother shook her head to warn him not to make any noise. He tiptoed across the room and put his lips close to her ear.

"Everything's closed down at City Hall because it's Saturday," he whispered.

She nodded and he started to ask her if it was all right if he went on looking for the truck. But Liza jerked awake and his mother waved him on out of the room. He couldn't wait around. The sooner he got to Si the better.

He stopped by the clothes closet in the entrance hallway and got his roller skates. They were not much when it came to transportation, but they were better than nothing. It was four long blocks to the boulevard, all downhill. He had to keep braking with his left foot to keep from running wild.

He found Si Bartlett at the Melrose Drive stop light. "Remember me?" Doug asked. "I'm the new crossing guard at Franklin School."

Si smiled and ran down the window. "Hi, Doug," he said. "Where's the fire?"

Doug had to pause a moment to catch his breath. "It isn't that bad," he said. "But I sure could use a little help."

Si listened with grave attention while Doug explained

about Liza's great loss. "This *is* serious," Si said. "We've got to act quickly before the whole City Council is involved."

He picked up his car telephone. "That you, Harry? Si here. One of our rubbish collectors made off with a little girl's doll buggy. . . . That's right and her dolls were in it. The name is Markel and the address is nine two six Cliffwood, that dead-end street below the dam. . . . Sure, I know, they work only a half day on Saturday. . . . Okay, let me know if you get any word. I'll probably be out at the dump." He leaned over and opened the door for Doug. "Hop in," he said. "We'll try our luck."

Doug sat extra tall in the patrol car. He hoped Si would use the siren and race through a red light or two, but of course Si did no such thing. The dump was south of town.

"All this land used to belong to a sand and gravel outfit," Si said. "They scooped out acres and now we're busy filling it in again."

They left the highway, and Si stopped the car where a number of dirt roads fanned out. "Likely all the trucks have dumped their loads by now," he said.

"Where?" Doug asked, looking out over the vast litterbug's paradise. "Which piles were dumped last?"

Si chuckled. "Where's your pioneer know-how?" he

demanded. "All you do is look for the freshest tire marks."

Doug got out of the car and walked to the rim of the dump. He looked out over the mounds of waste below him. If he lived to be a hundred, he still wouldn't have time to search through all that stuff. He was grateful for the breeze that carried away some of the smells.

As he stood there on the rim, it was as though he stood on high land at the seashore with countless waves of junk spread out below him. And there, in the midst of the sea was an old fellow with a long white beard.

Si waved a greeting to the man. "Hi, Skipper," he called. "How's the fishing?"

The skipper leaned on his short-handled rake and looked back at his pushcart that held a collection of tires and bottles and other valuable items. "Rags to riches," he said with a chuckle. "What brings you here?"

Si explained and asked where the last truck had dumped its load.

Skipper motioned farther on along the rim. "That pile of stuff with a mattress on top," he said. "Here, you can borrow my rake. I've got a full load as it is."

Doug had not raked long through that mountain of leaves and grass cuttings, paper and cans, before the sweat was stinging his eyes. With eighty million odds and ends buried out there it was silly to break his back trying to find one small doll buggy. It didn't make sense. He was thoroughly steamed up before Si shed his leather jacket and took over the raking.

Even Si had begun to slow down before he uncovered something that made him whistle. "Hey, what's this?" he called.

Doug stared as Si dragged out the battered doll buggy. He waded in where Si had been digging and searched around until he uncovered Emily. She looked as though she had been dipped in ashes, but she still wore her sappy smile.

"This does it," he said with satisfaction. "We can skip the other dolls. Emily is the only one that counts."

CHAPTER SEVEN **THE CHASE**

Sunday, when it was time to walk Buff, Stevie decided that he wanted to go along. Doug saw that there was a doctor and a nurse out on Mrs. Snead's front porch when they went past her house.

"I guess maybe Mrs. Snead is pretty sick," Stevie said. "My mom says it's her heart."

Doug nodded. "We've got to keep Buff quiet and we can't be gone long because it's supposed to rain."

"How about me holding the leash?" Stevie suggested, when they were halfway up the hill.

Doug shook his head. "He gets too frisky when we reach the jackrabbit country," he said. "No fooling, he'd just as soon kill a rabbit as not."

"He's sure big enough," said Stevie.

"And mean enough," said Doug.

"You sound like you don't like him," Stevie said.

"I sure don't," said Doug. "I wouldn't trust him as far as I can throw an elephant."

He began to whistle as soon as they reached the dirt road. "That's to warn the rabbits that old Killer Buff is on his way," he told Stevie.

"Buff probably thinks they're cats," said Stevie. "He sure won't let a cat in that yard of his."

Doug nodded sadly. "It's the killer in him," he said.

"Come on, let me hold the leash," Stevie begged. "I can manage him as good as you."

Doug held off until they could see the reservoir fence up ahead. They had failed to flush a single rabbit, and he was confident that his whistling was a fine warning system.

"Okay, take over," he agreed, handing the leash to Stevie. "I guess the rabbits have headed for the hills."

Stevie hadn't followed Buff more than fifty feet when a rabbit leaped out from the brush beneath a manzanita bush and bolted across the road in front of them. With a great heave Buff tore off after the rabbit. For a moment Stevie clung to the leash. He was airborne until he lost his grip and crashed to earth. Then, freed of Stevie's weight, Buff gained on the rabbit.

Doug chased after them feeling a sick horror as the rabbit zigzagged in long frantic leaps trying to escape Buff. In one last blind burst of speed the rabbit thumped into the fence and Buff was on top of it in a flurry of dust. The rabbit let out a frantic bleat of terror as Buff's jaws pinned him down. Doug raced to them expecting to find Buff tearing away at a bloody mess of bones and fur. But no, there stood Buff holding the rabbit down under his two front paws. Panting and excited, he peered over his shoulder at Doug with a look that said, "What do I do now?"

Doug caught his collar and pulled him to one side. The rabbit sprang up, his eyes bulging with fear, and skittered under the fence. His tall ears went erect as he raced away through the dry oats that grew on the far side.

A warm glow welled up in Doug as he went down on one knee and put his arms around Buff's neck. He hugged him close and felt his thumping heart and smelled his doggy wetness. Somehow he felt that Buff had spared him as much as he had spared the rabbit.

"Good boy," he said. "You did just fine."

Buff wriggled his delight and sat down on his haunches to show that he was willing to take more and more of such treatment.

Doug turned and grinned at Stevie. "Did you see that?" he cried. "Buff had that rabbit right between his jaws, and he let him go."

"Oh, the rabbit's okay," said Stevie. "I'm the one

who'll never be the same. When that rabbit screamed,
I thought he was a goner for sure."

"I know what you mean," Doug agreed. He eased
Buff's choke collar and gave him an affectionate pat.
"Good dog," he said.

"What's so good about him?" Stevie demanded. "If
you hadn't dragged him away, that rabbit would be
bunnyburger by now."

"I doubt it," said Doug. "He chases a tennis ball too,
but that doesn't mean he wants to eat it."

"Make up your mind," said Stevie, rubbing a skinned
place on his elbow. "One minute he's a killer, and the

next minute you try to make out he wouldn't hurt a flea."

Doug shrugged. "So I like him," he admitted. He felt a raindrop flick on the tip of his nose. "We'd better get on back home," he said. "Looks like the weatherman was right."

As they drew near their apartment building they saw that a group of people stood out in front of Mrs. Snead's house. "Hey, look," Stevie said, "that's an ambulance. They must be taking Mrs. Snead to the hospital."

They began to run, anxious to see what the two attendants had on the stretcher. But the whole stretcher was covered with a gray blanket, and the ambulance drove away before they got close enough for a good look.

They watched as Mrs. Markel came slowly down Mrs. Snead's front steps. She paid no attention to the raindrops that made dark dots on the sidewalk.

Doug ran up to her. "What happened?" he asked.

His mother scarcely glanced at him. "Mrs. Snead died," she said quietly. "She was very old and very tired." Buff crowded in on her to get a little attention. She motioned for Doug to take him on to the backyard. "Be sure to feed him and lock the gate."

Stevie frowned as he followed Doug. "I sure didn't know Mrs. Snead was *that* old," he said.

"This is going to be tough on Buff," Doug said. "I

guess I'd better prop the porch door open so he can get in out of the rain."

Stevie looked worried. "Who's going to feed him?" he asked.

Doug tapped himself on the chest. "Don't worry," he said. "There's a whole carton of dog food on the back porch and the can opener works just fine."

"Yeah, but he can't live all alone," said Stevie. "Who's going to walk him? Who's going to pay for his license? Who's going to take him to the vet's?"

Doug shrugged. "I guess maybe he'll go to the next of kin," he said. "They'll have to take care of all that."

"What do kin have to do with it?" Stevie asked.

"Mrs. Snead must have had some family to leave things to," said Doug.

"I never saw any," said Stevie.

"Well, neither did I," Doug had to admit. "At least none of them came to see her when she was sick."

"So, if there's no one to take Buff, what happens to him?" Stevie asked. "Does he get sent to the dog pound?"

Doug scowled at Stevie. "What kind of talk is that?" he demanded. "Buff's a fine dog with pedigree papers and all. Someone is bound to give him a good home."

"What someone?" Stevie asked. "Not you and not me. Dogs aren't allowed in our building."

Doug had no ready answer. He washed out Buff's

dish and gave him fresh water. He peered in through the glass panel of the kitchen door, but there was no one inside.

"I hate to leave him here alone," he admitted. "He sure could use a friend."

CHAPTER EIGHT   THE ORPHAN

Doug liked the rain. It poured all night and the next morning Mr. Markel drove Doug and Stevie to school. It was fun being crowded in the front seat, feeling all stiff and smelly in his new slicker and the yellow rain hat. It was exciting to have the rain drumming down just above their heads on the roof of the car, with the windshield wipers squeaking and the tires squishing on the wet streets.

He didn't like it so well when Chuck Nars caught up with him in the lower hallway at school, and asked, "Hey, what about my bike?"

Doug stared at him blankly. For the first time it occurred to him that he could no longer count on his money from Mrs. Snead. Now that she was gone, he doubted he could collect a cent for all that dog walking.

"I'm working on it," he said lamely, edging away.

Chuck planted himself squarely in front of Doug. "Don't try to give me the old runaround," he said. "When do I get my bike?"

Doug shrugged. "I'll try to let you know in a day or two," he promised.

Quickly he ducked around Chuck and hurried on to his classroom.

One thing Doug could say for Stevie, he never bothered to pussyfoot around. Rain or shine, when he had bad news, he let you have it all in a lump.

"I guess you may as well forget about joining the Secret Six," he told Doug, as they sloshed through the rain on their way home from school. "Chuck says you're a sneaky guy. He says it's not honest to give him the runaround the way you do."

"You think I like it?" Doug demanded. He stepped carefully into the rushing stream of water that ran flush with the curbing. He let it come up high on his boot, but not high enough to go over the top. "I wish he'd get off my back for five minutes till I can figure things out."

"Well, he won't," said Stevie, ducking his chin against a gust of rain. "He's going to beat you up the first chance he gets."

Doug began to steam under his raincoat. "It's not that simple," he said. "I'd be doing some swinging on my own."

Stevie peered at him with solemn interest. "Think you could lick him?" he asked.

"Sure, if I get mad enough," Doug said.

Stevie grinned, but then he gave up the enchanting idea with a shake of his head. "You jump on Chuck and you'll *never* get to join the Secret Six," he warned.

Doug raised his head and let the rain cool his hot face. Time was running out. How in the world was he going to get Chuck's bike fixed? He certainly had to think of something.

His mother met him at the front door of their apartment with a bath towel. He had to stand on newspapers while she mopped him off. He had barely got to the cooky jar when Stevie came pounding down the hallway and gave his special knock on the side door.

The moment Doug opened the door, Stevie pulled him outside and thrust the evening paper into his hand. "Look at that," he said. "I guess it's the end of good old Buff."

Right there on the front page was a picture of Buff. He looked wet and miserable and the flashlight on the photographer's camera had made his eyes look wild.

Doug felt his whole scalp tighten. "What happened?" he asked.

"Plenty," said Stevie. "Mrs. Snead wrote a letter to her lawyer and left everything she has to some animal

shelter. Her instructions say they have to put Buff to sleep on account of nobody would love him and take care of him the way she did."

"Good grief," said Doug.

He closed the door behind him. He didn't want Liza to get all worked up and ask a million questions when he didn't know any of the answers. He took the newspaper down the hallway to the back stairs where he could sit on a lower step and read without interruption. The caption under Buff's picture read, *It Shouldn't Happen to a Dog.*

"Mom heard it on the twelve o'clock news," said Stevie. "And right away the station was swamped with calls from people who wanted to save Buff. Five offered to give him a home."

"Then why all the worry?" Doug asked.

"They can't save him on account of the letter to the lawyer," said Stevie. His face was flushed and a watery look had come into his eyes. Apparently he considered Buff a goner. He acted as though Buff were some mongrel dog without a single friend in the world. He seemed to forget that Buff had Doug for a friend, a real friend.

Stevie leaned over Doug and pointed out a line near the end of the column. "See, the lawyer says he can save Buff until Mrs. Snead's estate is settled."

"Settled?" Doug asked.

"Yes," said Stevie. "The red tape part."

"So when will it be settled?" Doug asked.

Stevie shrugged. "We can ask someone," he said.

Doug shied away from the thought. "We'd better not," he said. "One word out of us and they'd get suspicious and say don't do this and don't do that, and then we'd be stuck."

"We're stuck anyway," said Stevie. "Someone's bound to come along from the animal shelter or the police department and walk off with Buff."

"Maybe he's already gone," Doug said in sudden alarm.

"Relax," said Stevie, "I saw him on his back porch just a few minutes ago."

"We've got to help him," Doug said. "We'll have to bring him over here and hide him in the basement."

Stevie began shaking his head before Doug finished speaking. "He can't just disappear," he objected. "The police would know better than that."

"We'll leave the gate open and for all they know he ran away."

Again Stevie's head wagged a no, no, no. "And who will they think left the gate open?" he asked. "You, of course, on account of everyone knows you're his dog walker."

"We'll hide him," Doug said.

"He's too big to hide," Stevie said.

"We'll have to keep him shut up in the storage room with the trunks and stuff."

Stevie looked more mournful than ever. "Someone's sure to hear him," he said.

"Not as long as all this rain is pouring down," said Doug. "You seem to forget he's been trained not to bark."

"He might forget himself," Stevie warned. "He gets real excited when it's time for his walk."

Doug started up. "It's that time right now," he said. "You coming along?"

"Mom wouldn't let me have my rain clothes," said Stevie. "She's drying them out in front of the oven."

Doug gave him the newspaper. "Okay," he said. "While I take Buff for his walk, you go down to the basement and open the side door so I can bring him in there when we get back."

"You're crazy," said Stevie. "What about his food and water?"

"I'll bring over his dog food, a few cans at a time," Doug said. "And you can bring over the sack of dog biscuits."

"You have a boat handy?" Stevie asked. "I told you Mom's riding shotgun on my boots and stuff."

"Go barefooted," Doug suggested.

"Sure, and step on glass or a nail and end up having to take a bunch of shots."

"So go to bed and forget the whole thing," said Doug in disgust, and he stalked on down the hallway to get his rain clothes.

When he went next door, he saw no one around. At least there was no one in the kitchen. Buff greeted him with eager whines. He seemed to think the rain was something special, made for his pleasure. On the walk he lunged along at a fast clip, planting his feet firmly as he waded the muddy water and jumping with confidence when he crossed the brownish flow where the gutters ran full.

His reddish gold coat turned a dark gleaming brown and his fine muscles rippled. Doug gave him an affectionate pat. "You look like a seal coming up for air," he said. Buff wriggled with pleasure and gave Doug's cold hand a quick warm lick to show how much he appreciated having a friend.

"Don't worry," Doug told him. "No one's going to take you away. After all, Mrs. Snead owed me money and that almost makes you part mine."

When they got back, they found that Stevie had left the side door of the basement open and he had managed to bring over the bag of dog biscuits and four cans of food. It was nice and warm in the basement with the automatic furnaces burning on low.

Doug wiped Buff off with a gunny sack and put him

in the storage room. Then he hurried next door to get the can opener and some extra cans of dog food. He was tempted to bring along Buff's bedding and his food and water bowls, but it wasn't likely that a runaway dog would take along his own bed and dishes. He still hoped those law people would think Buff had run away.

When he got back to the basement, Stevie was there with an old gray blanket for Buff's bed. "Got it from under my mattress," he said. "It was supposed to keep the springs from punching holes in it."

Doug stacked the dog food on the window ledge and got to work with the can opener.

"You know we're wasting our time," Stevie said. "Someone is sure to find Buff here."

Doug scowled at him. "Be sure you're not the big mouth who gives it away," he warned.

Stevie nodded. "I won't say a word," he promised. "I truly won't."

CHAPTER NINE

It rained three days and three nights. The following morning half the children stayed home from school and that half included Chuck Nars. Doug had a fine carefree day. Carefree, that is, until he and Stevie were returning home from school.

They had reached their own front walk when a man called to them from Mrs. Snead's front porch. They waited while he came out to speak to them.

"Don't blab all you know," Doug told Stevie, and he moved on a few steps leaving Stevie to do the talking.

"I'm trying to find Mrs. Snead's dog," the man said, smiling and friendly. "Have you seen him around here anywhere?"

"Sure, lots of times," said Stevie. "He was a good dog."

"When did you see him last?" the man asked.

"Yesterday," said Stevie.

"What time?" the man asked.

"About this time," Stevie said.

The man nodded to encourage Stevie. "What about this morning?" he asked. "Did you see him this morning?"

"No, I didn't," said Stevie.

The man glanced at Doug. "What about your friend?" he asked.

"Aw, he lives on the far side of the building," Stevie said. "He wouldn't see what goes on over on this side." He turned to join Doug who had been edging on toward his own front steps.

"I'll be staying in the Snead house from now on," the man called after them. "Let me know if you hear anything about the dog. There's a reward for anyone who returns him."

Stevie jerked to a stop. "Did you say reward?" he asked.

The man smiled. "Fifty dollars reward," he said.

Stevie followed Doug up the front steps. "Fifty bucks," he said in a dreamy voice. "Oh, boy! That would be twenty-five dollars for me and twenty-five dollars for you."

"Forget it," Doug said. "Even if we were low enough to turn Buff in, who's going to pay fifty bucks for a dog they plan to put to sleep?"

"Maybe it has something to do with the law," said Stevie. "Just think what you could do with twenty-five dollars. You could have Chuck's bike fixed right away and no hard feelings."

Doug's heart leaped at the thought. Stevie was pretty smart. He knew how much it would mean to Doug to get Chuck Nars off his back. "We can't chicken out on Buff," he said. "We've got to be fair."

Stevie tried to pretend the money meant nothing to him. "Don't look at me," he protested. "You and Chuck are the ones always arguing about that bike."

They stood dripping on the welcome mat at the front door. "How you going to sneak Buff out for his exercise?" Stevie asked. "That man next door is sure to be watching."

Doug pulled off his muddy boots and left them on the porch. "I'll think of something," he said. "I always do."

"Let me know what goes on," Stevie urged, as he started on down the hallway to his own apartment. "I'll be waiting."

Liza had the fidgets, because she'd had to stay in the house all day. Mrs. Markel asked Doug to take her out on the front porch where she could race up and down and chase her red beach ball. Watching Liza get all steamed up as she chased that ball gave Doug a fine idea for exercising Buff. But each time he took Liza back to the house, his mother said, "Not yet, Doug. I'll let you know when it's time to bring her in."

It was almost dark before Doug got rid of Liza. Then he hurried to Stevie's apartment and gave their special knock. Stevie came out in the hallway bringing the want-ad section of the *Evening Tribune*. "Hey, what kept you so long?" he asked. "I've been waiting and waiting to show you this." He pointed out a four-line advertisement in the Lost and Found column:

> *Boxer Male.* Reddish coat with white
> markings. Named *Buff.* $50 reward.
> No questions. BU 3–6119.

"There's the offer in black and white," he said. "That 'No questions' means we get our money and no fooling around."

Doug sighed. "Forget it," he said. "We've got to get Buff up to the roof for his exercise. It's flat up there with plenty of room." He showed Stevie the old tennis ball that he had brought along. "He'll chase this all over the place."

As they started off, the door opened and Stevie's mother called to him. "Remember, you're not to go out in this rain."

"I won't," Stevie promised. His mother closed the

door, but he seemed worried. "Suppose she pops out like that just as we get Buff halfway up the stairs?" he asked.

Doug shrugged. "We can take him up the back way," he said. "You be the lookout while I go get him."

"Hurry," said Stevie, "before some snooper comes along."

Doug found Buff chewing on a big soup bone and Doug reminded himself to thank Stevie for the offering. Buff was so glad to see him that he knocked him flat twice before they got to the basement stairs. Stevie made them stay back out of sight for a few wild moments until the tenant in Apartment 3 went out the front door. Doug had to hunch his shoulders and duck his head to keep Buff from licking his face as though he were a lollipop.

Stevie gave the all-clear whistle, and the three of them raced up the two flights of stairs to the roof. There was a night latch on the door, but they got it open without delay.

The rain beat down on the red sandy tar paper that covered the roof and streaked down the waist-high wall that enclosed the area. The boys crowded in the doorway, protected by an overhang that gave them a little shelter from the rain.

The moment Doug unsnapped the leash from Buff's

collar, the dog dashed out on the roof and began to race around and around as though he were caught up on a runaway merry-go-round. The wall around the roof was the only thing that kept him within bounds.

"Makes me dizzy just watching that dog," Stevie said.

Doug held up the tennis ball and whistled to Buff. The dog didn't slow down but, as he raced past, his eyes rolled Doug's way. The third time around he slowed down and Doug threw the ball for him to chase. Buff sprang in the air and caught the ball on the first bounce. He chewed down hard on it and trotted up to Doug, very pleased with himself. He retrieved the ball once; he retrieved the ball twice. The third time he refused to give up the ball. Doug had to twist it from his jaws before he could throw it again.

This time Buff jumped high and caught the ball in midair. By now his sides were heaving and his tongue dripping.

"It won't take much more of this to wear him down," Doug told Stevie. "Watch him go after this one."

Doug took a wide stance and threw the ball harder and farther than ever. It hit just once, took a wild bounce, and went over the wall.

Doug gasped in dismay. "No, no," he yelled, as Buff took off after the ball.

Buff paid no attention. He jumped after the ball, fleet

as a deer, and sailed over the side. There was a frantic yelp followed by a muffled crashing sound.

Doug and Stevie dashed to the spot where Buff had gone over the side. They leaned over the breast-high wall. Below them, two stories down, the acacia tree was swaying and heaving as though it were fighting a strong wind. Doug caught a glimpse of Buff. He was clawing and twisting as he tried to break his fall through the slippery leaves and the springy branches of the tree.

"Hold it," Doug yelled to him. "I'm coming."

He raced across the roof to the door. Stevie got in the way. "Did you see that take-off?" he demanded. "If I hadn't seen it with my own eyes, I'd never believe it."

Doug believed it all right. "Hurry!" he urged, as he pushed past Stevie. "He may be hurt."

Stevie kept up with him all the way down the stairs. But Stevie's mother popped her head out of the doorway as they ran past.

"Where do you think you're going?" she called.

Stevie had to turn back, but Doug dashed on outside and ran around to the side of the building. He was sure that he would find Buff stretched out cold and still under the acacia tree.

CHAPTER TEN   THE RUNAWAY

Doug splashed through the mud and water toward the acacia tree in time to see Buff stagger to his feet, duck his tail, and take off up the canyon road as though he were running from hot branding irons.

"Here, Buff," Doug called. "Here, boy."

Buff kept right on streaking through the rain, headed toward the reservoir. Doug didn't hesitate. He knew he had to get Buff back into the basement. He turned up the collar of his windbreaker and ran after Buff. Even though the dog was running wild, Doug felt sure the high wire fence at the Cliffwood Reservoir would stop him. By the time Buff reached the fence he would be so winded that he would have to slow down. By then he would be calm enough to recognize a friend and be glad to obey orders. After all, he was supposed to be a well-trained dog.

The rain slackened and Doug caught a glimpse of Buff as he floundered in a mudhole. Doug whistled, but Buff paid no attention. Doug stumbled into some mudholes of his own, and he moved over to the side of the road where the ground was decomposed granite and not so slippery. The road was a mess. It looked like a mountain stream, full of reddish mud and loose rocks.

The gate to the reservoir was kept tightly chained, but today the chain hung slack enough for Buff to squirm through the opening. He scampered off on the far side of the fence before Doug could reach him.

Doug was winded. He had a pain in his side, and there was an icy trickle of water dribbling down his back. "I've got to go back," he told himself. "I can't chase that crazy dog forever."

He tried a shrill whistle, but Buff kept on going. Doug caught a glimpse of him bobbing along through the low growth on the hillside. Panting and worried, Doug paused when he caught sight of all that gray water in the swollen lake. It gave him a spooky feeling to see so much water perched on the side of the mountain with nothing but that earthen dam to keep it in place.

"Hey, that's not a road," he yelled to Buff, as the dog took off across the abutment of the reservoir.

He had to admit that the broad rim of the dam did look like a road with its asphalt topping. Buff was halfway across the dam before he looked back over his shoulder to see if Doug was gaining on him. He stumbled in a hole or something that slowed him down. He seemed to be limping, and Doug dashed after him with renewed hope.

Doug jumped over the jagged break in the asphalt topping that had tripped Buff. He ran on twenty feet or more before he skidded to a stop. A crack in the dam! It couldn't be. There was always some official up here inspecting things.

Still, there was that break right there at his feet. Suppose that crack went down below the water line. Suppose it got wider and wider. What then? What was going to hold the lake in place if the dam gave way?

Cautiously he moved closer to the outer wall of the dam. He got down on both knees and peered over the side. All was gray mist and falling rain. He shivered under his soggy windbreaker and held his breath as he listened with all his senses. Faintly, above the patter of the rain, he heard a greedy gurgling sound. He leaned out far enough to see the reddish trickle of water that ran down the earthen wall below him. Short prickly waves shot up his spine as he crouched there, trying to decide what he should do.

"How come?" he asked himself, feeling alone and fearful. "Why isn't someone around here to stop this thing?"

He moved back from the edge and peered down

through the crack in the asphalt. He stared at the V-shaped opening. The rain-soaked earth was crumbling loose from the sides of the V and sliding into the escaping water. The cascade of reddish mud was not more than six inches wide, but at the rate it was going it would soon be a foot wide. Doug shuddered at the thought of that lake of water flooding the canyon. He looked around desperately. Somehow he had to stop that water.

He tried to kick dirt into the opening, but it held only

a moment before it swept over the side. He ran to the far hillside and uprooted clumps of grass and branches of brushwood to cram into the opening. It held only a moment before it washed away. Doug knew he had to get help. He was on the downhill trail before he remembered Buff. He stopped a moment and whistled, but there was no sign of life on the rain-misted hills.

"Hey, Buff," he yelled in desperation. "We've got to get out of here."

There was no sign of the dog, but Doug dared not wait another moment. He raced down the hill, cold and tense, his ear cocked, listening for the sound of water to rush down on him like an express train on the loose. The rain had slackened again, but the water in the road was getting deeper by inches. He stepped into a hole and fell on his hands and knees. He lost a shoe, but he dared not take the time to look for it.

A sharp pain was stabbing his side by the time he limped up the stairs to his own apartment. The door was locked. He pressed the bell a couple of times before he remembered to look under the mat for the key.

He opened the door. "Hey, Mom," he yelled.

There was no answer. He hurried to the kitchen and found a note propped up against the cooky jar. It read, "Daddy is taking Liza and me to market. Back soon. Mother."

Doug groaned. "Back soon," he cried. "Soon is too late."

He rushed out into the hallway, but there was no one in sight. He figured he didn't have time to knock on doors. He had to do something this minute. His thoughts darted around as jumpily as a kite in a high wind. "Cut it out," he warned himself. "This is one of those emergencies where you have to call the police."

He found the telephone book, but he couldn't even remember if the letter P came before or after the O. He dialed the operator. "This is an emergency," he cried. Then suddenly, with a warm feeling of relief, he remembered that he had a friend who would know what to do. "I have to speak to Si Bartlett at the police department," he said.

He did not get to speak to Si. The man at the police station listened to Doug's hurried story and asked for his telephone number, his address, and the exact location of the emergency.

"What was that name again?" he asked.

Doug could tell that the man thought he was some phony trying to turn in a false report. "Look, mister," he said desperately, "I'm a crossing guard at school, and you can depend on me. Si Bartlett is my friend."

"Fair enough," said the man briskly. "Watch for the patrol car and make your report."

Doug shoved his feet into his rain boots before he hurried outside. He saw that the water in the street was at least an inch higher than it had been when he went inside. His heart began to thump harder than ever when he heard the distant wailing of a siren. The sound grew louder and louder. Doug began to sweat. Suppose strange policemen answered his call! Suppose they didn't believe his story!

The police car sent out great fans of water as it raced up the hill toward him. For one anguished moment he wanted to run and hide for fear no one would believe him. As the police car came to a halt, a white truck with red lights flashing speeded past them and raced on up the canyon.

It was a serious Si Bartlett who rolled down the window to speak to Doug. "Was it you who reported trouble up ahead?" he asked.

"Yes, sir," Doug cried, his confidence restored at the sight of his friend. "There's a hole in the dam. The water is making it bigger and bigger every minute."

Si motioned for Doug to calm down. "That was one of the inspectors who just passed us," he said. "We'll follow him and see what's up."

The police car took off before Doug could ask Si to watch for Buff. There was a familiar beep on a horn as Mr. Markel drove in from the street. He eyed Doug with his let's-have-no-nonsense look. "What were the police doing here?" he asked.

Doug tried to explain what had happened. His mother and Liza leaned forward to hear what he was saying. Mr. Markel studied the reddish brown flow of water in the street. Quickly he drove on into the garage.

"We'll stay right here until we get a report," he said. "We may have to leave in a hurry."

A moment later the whole canyon was filled with a booming voice that came from the loudspeaker on the police car as it returned from the upper canyon. It was Si Bartlett's voice that blared the warning. "Don't panic, folks. There's a dam break up the canyon. Get to high ground at once. Do not delay. Warn your neighbors. I repeat. Get to high ground at once."

Mr. Markel got out of the car. "I'll be right back," he said. "I've got to warn the tenants."

Doug felt that he could never go off and leave Buff abandoned in the hills. Who would feed him? Who would see to it that he had a nice dry place to sleep? In the distance fire engines were clanging their way up the canyon. Sirens were wailing. The constant blare of Si's loudspeaker made it hard to think clearly, but Doug figured he could hurry and try to beat his dad back to the car.

Without a word to anyone he darted away, heading up

the canyon. The flood water had edged up over the sidewalk by now; it was almost ankle-deep on his boots.

"Hey, kid," some man yelled to him, "you're headed the wrong way. Get on back to your folks."

"Yes, sir," Doug called back. "Just a moment."

Give him another five minutes or so and he was sure he could find Buff. Surely the dog had sense enough to retrace his own steps when he found that he was lost. Doug's boots were heavy and awkward, but he kept running until he reached the end of the cement paving. There a great fan of muddy water shot high into the air. The dirt road had washed out leaving a hole that must be four or five feet deep. The pavement still held firm and divided the stream into two separate channels that ran on either side of the street.

Doug kept to the rocky hillside as he hurried along the stream. "Here, Buff," he yelled, trying to make himself heard above the roar of the water. "Here, boy."

Presently an excited "Woof" answered him. There, on the far side of the stream, was Buff, racing up and down the bank, eager to get to Doug but afraid of that water.

"No, no," Doug yelled, motioning with an open palm for Buff to go back away from the stream. "Stay on that side till we get down below."

He turned away and started back the way he had come to give Buff the idea. But when he glanced back, the dog was gone. Doug looked searchingly all along the far side of the stream. No dog. Doug hesitated. He knew he ought to hurry back down the canyon. Every moment the flood water was creeping higher. He had no choice; he had to get out of there. Whistling one last time, he turned away. Then he saw a dark object plunging in midstream. At first it looked like a small blackened stump. Doug went upstream to get a closer look.

"Buff!" he yelled, seeing that the dog was trying to swim upstream against the current. He rode high in the water paddling furiously. Apparently he didn't know enough to let the water carry him along until he could angle his way to the nearest solid ground.

Doug shouted and clapped his hands to attract the dog's attention. Buff's big brown eyes bulged with fear as he struggled against the pull of the water. The floating limb of a tree rolled him over. His head went under.

Doug plunged into the swirling water, boots and all. For a moment he floundered helplessly, all but choked by the chin strap on his rain hat. He was carried twenty feet downstream before he managed to hang onto Buff's collar. Together they were swept into the deeper water where the pavement began. Doug's toes could barely touch bottom. He managed to hook one arm over the edge of the cement and hung there, his boots full of water, each foot as heavy as lead. He struggled to get

Buff up on the cement where the water was only a foot or so deep. Turning and twisting, tugging and pushing, he kept trying to lift Buff to safety. Buff didn't get the idea. He was choking and gasping, fighting to free himself from the grip on his collar. Doug's elbow kept slipping and his boots kept dragging at him. He would never make it. Never.

Dimly he heard his father's voice. "Hold on, Doug," he shouted. "I'm coming."

Mr. Markel was only a wavery blur to Doug as he waded out, leaning against the rush of the water. There were two men with him. Each man gripped the wrist of his companion, forming a human chain. Mr. Markel reached far out and grabbed the collar of Doug's jacket.

He hauled Doug up on the cement, and Doug hauled Buff along too. Wheezing and coughing, Buff made it to the sidewalk on his own wobbly legs.

Doug put his arms around the dog's neck and gave him a hug. "Good boy," he whispered. "You're a fighter all the way." Buff gave Doug's hand a quick lick and wagged his short tail. The whole experience, he seemed to say, was just another fine adventure that they shared together.

Mr. Markel hurried them to the car. "Quick, Doug. Get that mutt inside. We've got to get out of here."

CHAPTER ELEVEN **THE FLOOD**

Mr. Markel had brought some blankets from the apartment. He spread them out on the back seat for Doug and Buff. Before Doug could pull the blankets around them, Buff managed to shake himself. Flicks of water went over everyone. But no one paid any attention. They were too busy watching what went on around them. Most of the neighbors were running here and there, shouting questions at the dozens of firemen and policemen who had rushed into the canyon.

Carefully Mr. Markel started to back out of the garage. Doug saw that Stevie and his parents were in their car out in the middle of the street, but they were not going anyplace. They were stalled behind two other cars that were locked bumper to bumper. A tow truck was trying to get the two cars out of there, but someone's garage had floated off its foundation and blocked the way. Beyond the floating garage a manhole that was in the middle of the street blew its top and a great geyser of muddy water shot up into the air.

Mr. Markel did not say a word. He just backed a few inches and pulled forward a few inches, repeating the shifting over and over again as though he were in a tight spot on a parking lot. Gradually he managed to jockey the car out on the sidewalk where nothing blocked his way except a lot of frantic people. He drove cautiously with the two left wheels of the car on the cement side-walk and the outer wheels on the grass of the parking strip.

"Hope we can turn left at the first side street and get out of this," he said.

As they crept past Mrs. Snead's house, Doug saw that the water covered her front yard. When they reached the corner, a policeman with a red flashlight waved for them to turn left. They mowed down a stop sign as they jolted down over the curbing, but the policeman waved them on. The motor conked out. The current caught the car and skidded it along sideways until it banged into a stalled car that was full of yelling people.

Liza began to scream. Buff barked and Doug reached for the door handle. "Let's get out of here," he cried.

"Stay where you are," said Mr. Markel sternly. He rolled down the window and stuck out his head. "How about a tow?" he called to the policeman with the red flashlight.

The policeman nodded and waved to the men on a big red truck who were backing down the hill toward them. The men hooked a steel cable to the front bumper of the Markels' car. Then they slowly towed it toward the top of the hill. A man who looked like a fire chief, because of the gold emblem on the front of his cap, called to Mr. Markel, "Get moving, friend. You're blocking the way."

Mr. Markel stepped on the gas. The engine sputtered a time or two and then started up. He drove on to the top of the hill. There three policemen were trying to keep curious people back out of the way. One of the policemen cleared a space where Mr. Markel could park the car, a narrow slot back of a white guardrail.

"You'd best sit it out here till we get this traffic snarl cleared away," he said.

People crowded in around the car. All of them were staring down into the canyon. Most of the people were out by now, but Doug saw a little girl he knew at school being carried out of her apartment house on the back of a fireman. Water was sweeping across the porch of the little white house on the corner. Presently the roof of the porch began to sag and a few minutes later the roof crashed down in a great splash of water.

"Think what all that mud and water is doing to the stores down on the boulevard," said Mrs. Markel.

Suddenly the big air-raid siren that was tested every third Friday at ten thirty began to blast off. Doug almost jumped out of his skin. It was some kind of a signal. All the fire trucks and police cars got out of the canyon in a hurry.

"Here she comes," some man shouted.

There was a frightful roaring in the air, and the people fell quiet as they listened. Buff crouched down and Doug put his hands over his ears. Shivering and afraid he pressed his face against the window. He saw the great wall of reddish water boom down the canyon. It carried a load of uprooted trees and brush, automobiles and garbage cans, roof sections and huge slabs of building materials that rode the crest for a time before they plunged out of sight.

Little by little the force of the flood spent itself, but they sat there for an hour or more watching the undermined houses cave in, the big granite boulder bash the battered cars, and the telephone poles shake and topple over. It was worse than some horror picture that goes on and on.

Secretly Doug was glad when Liza began to cry and his mother said, "Can't we get away from here?"

Mr. Markel appealed to the nearest police officer. "Think you can get us out of here?" he asked. "I've got to find a place for my family to sleep."

Liza stopped crying the moment the car started. "Now where are we going?" she demanded in a loud voice.

No one answered. Doug pushed Buff out of the way so he could get a last look out the steamy back window as they drove away.

"I'd never believe it unless I'd seen it with my own eyes," he said.

Liza squirmed around in the front seat and stared at

him with red-rimmed eyes. "You said we weren't going to move from our apartment," she said crossly. "You told a big story."

Doug sank back in his corner, one arm around Buff. "Don't look at me," he protested. "This flood wasn't my idea."

DOUG
AND
BUFF

CHAPTER TWELVE

Mr. Markel drove them to a new motel on Twenty-fourth Street. "We'll stay here until we see how bad Cliffwood was hit," he said.

The man who owned the motel pointed to the *No Pets Allowed* sign. "Seeing as how this dog is a refugee from a flood," he said, "I guess we won't object as long as you let him sleep in the car."

As soon as everyone had cleaned up, Mr. Markel tried to take his family to Weldon's Cafeteria to eat, but they found the boulevard was closed to all traffic. A river of mud had swept down from Cliffwood and spilled into the stores and piled up all along the street. Doug got a good look at the two big city graders that were busy scooping up mud and dumping it into trucks that hauled it away.

They ate at a little restaurant over on a side street and

Doug was allowed to order steak and French-fried potatoes. He saved the T-bone from his meat and had it put into a paper bag for Buff.

When they returned to the motel, Mrs. Markel took Liza inside as there were two men waiting to speak to Mr. Markel. They seemed to be in a great hurry.

"I'm Bill Brooks from the *Morning Tribune*," said the tall thin one. "Is this the boy who reported the break in the dam?"

"That's right," said Mr. Markel.

"Si Bartlett gave us your name," said the reporter. "We've been chasing all over town trying to find you." He turned to Doug, who was trying to fend off Buff. Buff had been fed, but he knew there was something choice in that greasy paper bag.

"Can you get your dog to hold still a minute while we get a picture?" the reporter asked.

Doug glanced at his father. Mr. Markel nodded his consent, and Doug knelt down and drew Buff close. "Sit," he said sternly. Buff obeyed, though he quivered with impatience.

The photographer's bright flashlight went off before Doug remembered that Buff was supposed to be lost.

"Hold it," said the photographer. "Let's get another."

Doug pulled Buff back into the shadows behind the car, where he couldn't be seen as clearly. The reporter followed them. "What happened up there at the dam?" he asked.

Doug figured he had to avoid mentioning Buff. "I'd rather not talk about it," he said, careful to be polite.

The flashlight blinded him again, but Buff was in the shadows sniffing at the paper bag.

"Could it be that you're worrying about that no trespassing sign at the dam?" asked the reporter with a smile.

"Not exactly," said Doug. "The gate was open wide enough for Buff to get through, and I had to get him back."

The reporter made a note on a pad of paper. "Buff?"

he said. "Isn't that the lost dog that belonged to Mrs. Snead?"

Doug ducked his head. "Yes, sir," he admitted. "But she wanted him put to sleep and that's not fair."

"Don't worry," said the reporter. "After this story breaks, I can practically guarantee you'll get to keep the dog."

"Maybe not," said Doug, not sure that his folks would let him keep Buff. "But I'll sure find a good home for him."

"Fair enough," said the reporter. He glanced at his notes. "How big was the break in the dam when you first saw it?" he asked.

Doug held his hands about two feet apart.

"Didn't it occur to you to try to stop it then and there?" the reporter asked.

"I tried," said Doug. "But the sides were caving in so fast I figured it was best to call the police."

"You called the police?" the reporter asked.

"Yes," Doug said. "Then we threw a bunch of stuff in the car and got out of there."

The reporter nodded. "Some weren't so lucky," he said. "Houses caved in and cars piled up. Still, no lives were lost as far as we know."

"How about the two-story apartment building in the nine hundred block?" Mr. Markel asked.

"It was too dark to see much," said the reporter. "The worst is over by now, but no one is allowed in the area. Maybe you can get a look in the morning. Thanks a lot for the story."

The two men hurried off, and at long last Buff was allowed to tear into the paper bag.

The next morning the sun came out faint and misty. "Get your boots on," Mr. Markel told Doug. "We'll drive over to Cliffwood and take a look around."

It was not a very close look. They had to park the car two blocks away. Curious people were milling around all over the place, and barriers had been set up at all the cross streets that led to Cliffwood Road. Mr. Markel showed his driver's license to the police officer who guarded the nearest barrier, and they were allowed to walk on through. Doug was soon in mud that sucked and pulled at his boots, but most of the water had disappeared.

They were still half a block from their own building when his dad walked out on a retaining wall that looked good and solid. It was all that was left of the corner house. In front of the house the pavement had been washed out in huge slabs; the whole street looked like one huge sloppy excavation.

"This is as far as we go," said Mr. Markel.

Doug saw that the walls of the house across the street

had caved in. The roof had floated away and the car was sandwiched in between the layers of the garage.

"Hey, that's Chuck's house," he yelled to make himself heard above the roar of the Caterpillar that was working in the street below them. "They may as well haul it off to the city dump."

Nothing looked familiar. Most of the trees had been uprooted, even the electric light standards had toppled over.

Mr. Markel pointed up the street. "There's our building high and dry," he said. "Lucky we were on higher ground."

Suddenly Doug remembered his pet turtle. "I guess we lost Chester," he said with a twinge of sorrow. "His marker bush is gone."

"You may find him," said Mr. Markel. "A turtle is a good swimmer."

"I'll get Stevie to help me hunt for him as soon as things dry out," Doug said.

Mr. Markel started back to the car, but Doug lingered to watch the big Caterpillar work. "Come along," said his dad. "We've got to get breakfast before you go to school."

"School!" Doug couldn't believe anyone would expect him to waste his time at school when there was so much excitement going on right here on Cliffwood. "They won't have school on a day like this."

Mr. Markel motioned him back toward the car. "The disaster here doesn't mean a thing to the rest of the district," he said. "You'll have school as usual."

Before they went into the restaurant to get breakfast, Mr. Markel gave Doug a dime to put in the coin box on the rack that held copies of the *Morning Tribune*. There, staring out from the left-hand corner of the front page, was a big picture of Doug and Buff.

The wording under the picture read, "Hero in action. Doug Markel and his dog, Buff, were quick to alert residents of the Cliffwood Reservoir disaster." There was a column headed, "Fast Action Saves Life and Property." And Bill Brooks's name was there to show who wrote it. Doug stood still and read the whole thing straight through. He didn't know his dad was standing behind him until Mr. Markel said, "Well, Son, how does it feel to be a hero?"

"Okay, I guess," Doug said. But he was worried. "I hate to see that picture of Buff. Suppose Mrs. Snead's lawyer comes to claim him?"

Mr. Markel took the paper from Doug. "I think the case is coming to Judge Mead first," he said.

Doug felt a quivery sensation inside, a reckless sort of feeling. "If you were someone important and a kid phoned you and asked you a favor about a dog would you get mad?"

Mr. Markel shrugged. "Not if I had five kids and four dogs," he said.

Doug squirmed. "Does Judge Mead have five kids and four dogs?" he asked.

Mr. Markel reached in his pocket and drew out a dime, which he gave to Doug. He nodded toward the glass-enclosed telephone booth that stood at the corner. "Why don't you find out?" he suggested.

Doug took the coin and ran to the telephone booth. He had to act quickly before he lost his nerve. The telephone directory gave an office number and a home number for Judge Mead. Doug dialed the home number and made himself stand there until he heard the judge's hearty voice.

"This is Doug Markel," he said hurriedly. "I have been taking care of Mrs. Snead's dog, walking him and feeding him and all that. So she owes me this money and I thought maybe you'd let me keep the dog and call it quits."

The last word trailed off in a whisper, but Judge Mead had heard every word. "Well now," he said. "I was just reading about you and that dog in the morning paper. Do you have a suitable home for him?"

"Oh, yes," said Doug. "It's suitable for me too."

"I see," said Mr. Mead. "What do your parents think about a dog in the family?"

"They think it's fine," said Doug recklessly.

"Hm," said Judge Mead. "As long as Mrs. Snead was willing to place her dog in your care, I'm sure you are a responsible young man. The dog is yours."

Doug let out a joyous yelp. "Oh, thank you," he said, and he thumped the receiver back on its hook and tore out of there. "He's mine!" he yelled to his father. "Buff is all mine."

Mr. Markel opened the door of the restaurant for Doug. "Don't forget to pull the ripcord as you drift back to earth," he said. "This promises to be a day to remember."

Doug never did know what he ate for breakfast. It must have been good, because he finished in a hurry and was on the school grounds long before the second bell rang.

Stevie came running to meet him. He had on one blue sock and one red sock, but other than that he looked about the same as usual. "Yah, hero for a day," he called out. "The big shot with his picture in the paper and all that stuff."

Doug did not mind anything Stevie said, but he tightened up when he saw Chuck Nars hurrying toward them. Chuck was trailed by a bunch of kids and he looked as big and bossy as ever.

"Hi," he called to Doug, as though it hurt him to be so

friendly. "Mrs. Phelps wants you to come to her office right away. Some reporter from the *Evening Herald* wants to talk to you."

Mrs. Phelps was principal of the school, but Doug doubted she knew anything about him. "You sure it's *me* she wants?" he asked.

Chuck nodded impatiently. "Who else?" he demanded. "The reporter wants Stevie and me along, so we can tell him how it feels to be caught in a flood."

Stevie shuddered. "I can tell him plenty," he said. "I was scared stiff."

Doug backed off. "I told a reporter all I know," he said.

"This is a different paper," Chuck assured him. "Come on. We're all in this together."

"Yeah, together," said Stevie. He caught Chuck's arm and held him back a moment. "Tell Doug how the guys in the Secret Six voted," he urged.

Chuck's face puckered up as though he tasted a sour lemon. "I don't know what's wrong with those fellows," he told Doug. "They want to make the Secret Six the Secret Seven, and you're it."

Dimly Doug saw the smiling faces around him. Still, he had to face up to Chuck. "I don't know when I'll get your bike fixed," he admitted.

Chuck looked more disgusted than ever. "I have news for you," he said. "Your bike washed away with my other stuff. No matter how you look at it, I owe you a bike."

Doug tried to take it all in. Chuck's bike was his bike, and the Secret Six wanted him to make it the Secret Seven. And Buff was his dog for keeps!

MAURINE H. GEE was born in Missouri and educated in State College, New Mexico. She has traveled widely—on this continent, in South America, Europe, Hawaii, the Orient, the Middle East, and the Near East. She is married, and has two married daughters. At present she lives in Beverly Hills, California. She has been a Parent-Teacher Association board member and a leader of a Girl Scout troop, and now does volunteer work in a children's hospital. An outdoors enthusiast, she and her husband have made fishing trips ranging from Reindeer Lake in Canada to Lake Nahuel Haupi in Argentina.